KB180875

한국 희곡 명작선 07

어른아이

한국 희곡 명작선 07

어른아이

최세아

평민사

죄
세
아

어른아이

등장인물

송희주(29세, 여)
유미리(26세, 여)
아버지(57세) : 송희주의 아버지
최 PD(48세, 남)

때

계절이 바뀌는 시기.

무대

오피스텔 내부.
(웹툰) 작업 책상과 식탁이 있다.
책상 위에 놓인 액자에는 중년 여성의 사진이 있다.
거실 전체를 비추는 거울이 주방 쪽에 있다.
현관으로 등장인물들의 등퇴장이 가능하다.

어둠속에서 클랙슨 소리, 요란하게 울린다.
클랙슨 소리 잦아들면 송희주, 〈섬집 아기〉를 부르며 등장.
흰 락카로 바닥에 사람 모양(시체 윤곽선)을 마킹한다.
다 그리면 그림 안에 눕는다.

송희주 엄마… 엄마의 죽음 위로 수많은 자동차 바퀴들이 달린
다. 망각은 신이 준 축복이라지만 기억하고 싶은 나에
겐 끔찍한 형벌이다.

순간 강렬한 헤드라이트가 쏟아지면서 클랙슨 소리 높아진다.
잠깐의 암전.

무대 밝아지면,
사진 속의 중년 여성과 같은 옷, 같은 머리를 한 유미리, 식사
준비를 하고 있다. 주방용 저울에 음식을 정확히 계량하면
서… 무대 중앙에서는 송희주가 요가 동작을 하고 있다.
송희주의 시선이 자꾸 핸드폰으로 간다.

유미리 (거울을 통해 송희주를 보며) 자세 똑바로 해. 그래야 라인
이 예뻐져.

'딩동' 문자 도착 소리.
송희주, 동작을 멈춘다.

유미리   (시계를 보며) 아직 시간 남았어.

송희주, 핸드폰을 확인한다.

유미리   10분 채우라니까.

송희주   쉬고 싶어요.

유미리   조급해 한다고 발표가 일찍 나진 않아.

송희주   … 떨어졌대요.

유미리   (돌아보며) 전화 왔니?

송희주   문자.

유미리, 주방에서 거실로 오며…

유미리   이유가 뭐라니?

송희주   몰라요.

유미리   그러면 안 되지.

유미리, 핸드폰으로 전화를 한다.

유미리   (통화하며) 〈오늘의 웹툰상〉 담당자 좀 부탁합시다. (사이) 나, 수상후보 작가 송희주 엄마예요.

송희주   지금 뭐하는 거예요, 엄마?

유미리   (통화하며) 이번에 우리 딸이 떨어졌더군요. 적어도 심사 기준은 알려줘야 하는 거 아닌가요? 문자로 딕. 최소한 예의는 갖춰서 통보를 하더라도 해야죠. (사이) 듣기 싫고. 어디 심사 기준이나 들어봅시다. (사이) 말하기 곤란하면 심사위원 전화번호를 주든가. 여보세요! 여보세요? (전화를 끊으며) 형편없는 것들.

송희주 뭐래요?

유미리 신경 쓸 거 없어. 보석을 못 알아보는 거지. 멍청한 것들. 밥 먹자.

유미리, 주방으로 가서 음식을 식탁으로 옮긴다.
송희주, 식탁 의자에 앉는다.

유미리 그깟 일로 기죽을 필요 없어. 무게감 있는 상도 아니었잖니.

송희주 … 연어 먹고 싶어요.

유미리, 맞은편 의자에 앉는다.

유미리 방사능 때문에 당분간 생선은 식탁에 올리지 않을 거야. (닭 가슴살을 먹기 좋게 찢어주며) 단백질, 탄수화물, 지방, 칼슘, 비타민 5대 영양소, 하루 권장 섭취량까지 다 맞췄으니까 남기지 말고 꼭꼭 씹어 먹어.

송희주, 식사를 한다.

물에 손이 간다.

유미리 (부드럽지만 단호하게) 식사 도중에 마시는 물은 소화 장
애를 일으키게 한다고 얘기 했지?

송희주 퍽퍽해서…

유미리 한번이 두 번 되고, 두 번은 습관으로 자리 잡는 법이야.
나중에 병원 신세 지면서 후회하지 말고 엄마 말 들어.

송희주, 물 대신 샐러드를 먹는다.

유미리 (숟가락에 닭 가슴살을 올려주며) 지난번에 배경으로 사용
할 로터리 사진 필요하다고 했지? 그거 지역별로 찍어
서 스크랩 해뒀다. 책꽂이에 꽂아뒀으니까 식사 마치고
확인해.

송희주 (익숙하다는 듯) 네.

유미리 아! 최 PD한테 전화 왔길래 1시간 후에 하라고 했다.
속없이 다 풀어내지 말고 짧게 말하고 끊어. 직장 상사
랑은 적당한 거리를 두는 게 좋아. 너무 멀면 네가 있는
지 없는지도 모를걸. 그렇다고 너무 가까우면 넘지 말
아야 할 선을 넘을 수 있어. 사적인 친밀감이 공적인 영
역을 침범하면 예의 없음으로 비춰질 수 있다는 걸 명
심하렴.

송희주   알고 있어요.

유미리   내일 마감이지?

송희주   엄마가 나보다 더 잘 알잖아요.

유미리   얼마나 남았어?

송희주   채색만…

유미리   봐. 엄마 말 들으니 얼마나 좋아. 하루에 세 시간씩 꾸준히 하니까 마감에 쫓길 일 없지, 밤샐 일 없으니까 피부가 이렇게 좋잖아. 피부 좋아진 것 좀 봐. 네가 봐도 그렇지?

송희주   어제 마사지 받았잖아요.

유미리   (무시하고) 단행본 계약 건, 모레 오전으로 잡았다. 대표가 늦는 거 싫어하는 사람이야. 30분 일찍 도착할 예정이니까 거기에 맞춰서 준비하도록 해.

송희주   이번에도 내 의사는 중요하지 않네요.

유미리   네가 엄마 말 들어서 손해 본 거 있니? 내가 널 키우면서 딱 한번 후회한 건 네가 하고 싶다는 이 일, 하게 한 거다. 네가 선택한 일이니까 내 앞에서 힘들다고 징징대지 마. 이왕 시작한 거 끝을 봐야지. 그렇게 바닥에 빌빌거리는 꼴 보려고 어릴 때부터 친구 만들어주고, 이 학원 저 학원으로 실어 나르며 성적 올려주고, 새벽부터 줄 서가며 도서관 자리 맡아가면서 있는 돈, 없는 돈 다 들여서 먹이고 입힌 줄 알아? 내가 왜 그렇게 했겠니? 다 너 잘 되라고. 나처럼 살지 말라고. (머리를 쓰다듬으며) 제대로 돌려놓을 거다.

송희주, 숟가락을 내려놓는다.

송희주   (읊조리듯이) 엄마한테 난 실패작이구나.

유미리   실패라는 말 함부로 하는 거 아니야. 아직 끝나지 않았어. 내가 그렇게 안 둬.

송희주   (일어나며) 조금만 쉴게요.

유미리   마감이 코앞인데?

송희주   (거실로 가며) 그러고 싶어요.

유미리, 식탁을 치우며…

유미리   그럼 그렇게 해.

송희주, 유미리를 빤히 쳐다본다.
유미리, 본래 자신의 말투로.

유미리   가서 쉬어. 쉬라고.

송희주   (표정이 싸늘해지며) 우리 엄마는 그러지 않았어.

유미리   아니… 그게… 피곤하다고 하니까… 잠깐 쉬어도 문제 될 거 없어 보이길래…

송희주   내가 당신에게 돈을 주고 고용한 이유는 우리 엄마처럼 행동하라는 거지, 당신 생각을 집어넣어서 마음대로 지껄여도 좋다는 뜻이 아니야.

유미리 이해가 안 돼. 사실, 나도 돈 받고 하는 일이니까 네가 하라는 대로 돈 받은 만큼만 하면 그만이야. 하지만 너 보면 좀 답답하고 숨 막혀. 엄마가 시키는 대로 사는 거 너도 힘들어 하잖아. 그런데 왜 이 짓을 계속하려는 거야?

송희주 우리 거래는 끝난 것 같다.

송희주, 방으로 들어간다.

유미리 내 말은 너도 어른이니까 네 생각대로 해보라는 거지.

송희주, 방 안에서…

송희주 (소리) 끝났다고 했지. 가.

유미리 (혼잣말로) 당장 있을 데도 없는데… (방문을 향해) 그래, 알았어. 잘하면 되잖아. 그래도 계약은 계약인데 끝까지 해. 너 나만한 사람 만나기 쉬운 줄 알아?

송희주, 반응 없다.

유미리 (엄마의 말투로) 희주야, 문 열어. 엄마 말 안 들어?

여전히 방안에 있는 송희주는 반응이 없다.

이때, '딩동' 차임벨 소리.

여러 번, 빠르고 거칠게.

유미리 (인터폰 보면서 엄마 말투로) 누구세요?

최 PD (격앙된 목소리로) 문 열어, 송작가.

유미리 누군지부터 말해요.

최 PD 지금 초짜 티내? 열어, 당장.

유미리 글쎄 누군지 먼저 밝히라고요!

송희주, 방을 나온다.

최 PD, 현관을 손으로 두드린다.

유미리 (엄마 말투로) 교양 없기는. 상대하지 마라.

송희주 (인터폰을 보고) 같이 일하는 PD야.

유미리 걱정 마. 잘할게.

송희주 잘 하지 말라고. 들키고 싶지 않아.

송희주, 문을 열어준다.

최 PD, 등장.

최 PD (버럭) 대체 일을 어떻게 하는 거야?

송희주 …

유미리   (엄마 말투로) 어휴, 무식해.

최 PD   누구? … 나?

송희주, 유미리를 제지한다.

최 PD, 송희주와 유미리를 번갈아 바라본다.

송희주   (재빨리 유미리에게) 과일 좀.

유미리, 주방으로 간다.

최 PD   (유미리를 아래위로 훑어보며) 취향 참. 순간 송작가 어머닌가 했네.

송희주   친척 동생이에요. (말을 돌리며) 아직 마감날 아닌데… 다음 작품 때문에 오셨어요?

최 PD   다음? 이런 식으로 하는데 다음이 어딨어? 다음이!

최 PD, 가지고 온 인쇄물을 꺼낸다.

최 PD   (가리키며) 여기 (넘겨서) 여기 (넘겨서) 여기 (넘겨서) 여기

송희주, 인쇄물을 보고 있다.

유미리, 과일을 깎으면서 거울로 거실 상황을 지켜본다.

최 PD	수정하라고 했는데 그대로 둔 이유가 뭐야?
송희주	…
최 PD	송작가. 내가 지금 선생님 모시고 일하나?
송희주	(눈치 못 채게 아주 살짝 고개만 가로젓는다)
최 PD	스토리에도 안 맞아, 시대도 어긋나, 작품에 꼭 필요한 복선도 아니야. 회마다 이 시체 윤곽선을 고집하는 이유가 대체 뭐냐고 묻잖아.
송희주	…
최 PD	내가 우스워?
송희주	…
최 PD	사람이 물으면 대답을 좀 해!
송희주	…
최 PD	아, 됐고. 네티즌들 작가 정신병자라고 중지 시키라는데 어쩔 거야? 지금 직원들이 전체 비상이야. 송작가 하나 때문에.
송희주	…
최 PD	고집을 피웠을 때에는 뭔가 이유가 있겠지. 이도저도 아니면 엿 한 번 먹어봐라, 이거던가.
송희주	…
최 PD	애들 장난하는 것도 아니고.

최 PD, 인쇄물로 송희주의 어깨를 툭툭 치면서…

최 PD   어른이면 어른답게 굴어.

최 PD, 잡고 있던 인쇄물을 바닥에 버린다.
낱장으로 된 종이가 떨어져 흐트러진다.
송희주, 표정이 굳는다.

최 PD   이 시체윤곽선, 어머니 맞지? 돌아가신 분을 왜 자꾸
그려? 소름끼치게. 이제는 정신 좀 차리자. 응?

송희주   …

최 PD   나 정도 되니까 작가 체면 생각해서 이 정도로 끝내
는 줄 알아. 다른 PD 같았으면 쓰레기통에 쳐 박고도
남았어.

송희주, 쪼그려 앉아서 떨어진 인쇄물을 주워 모은다.
최 PD, 인쇄물을 발로 밟아 짓이긴다.
송희주, 수치심에 떨지만 고개 숙인 채 가만히 있다.
최 PD, 그대로 앉으며 송희주와 눈높이를 같이 맞춘다.

최 PD   (송희주의 턱을 들어올리며) 딴 짓하지 말고 돈 벌자고 돈.

송희주   …

최 PD   신인이 고분고분 해야지. 별 거 있는 줄 알아? 이 바닥
에서 크고 싶으면 내 말대로 해.

송희주   …

최 PD　(일어나며) 허투루 듣지 마. 작가 대접은 오늘까지니까.

최 PD, 바닥에 흐트러진 인쇄물을 발로 찬다.

최 PD　버려, 이딴 거.

유미리, 과일을 챙겨오다가 이 상황에 쟁반을 놓친다.

유미리　(엄마 말투로) 어디서 이따위 몰상식한 짓을… 창작의 창자도 모르는 인간이 PD를 하니 그 회사도 오래 못 가겠네.

최 PD　뭐!… 뭐?

유미리　이 시간에 여기 와서 작가를 들들 볶을 게 아니라 표현의 자유도 모르면서 떠들어대는 독자들이나 관리하세요. 알아들어요?

최 PD　떽! 어디서 어른을 가르치려고 들어?

유미리　어머, 내 눈엔 어른으로 안 보이는데 어쩌면 좋아요. 어른이면 어른답게 잘못된 게 있으면 좋은 말로 가르치고 타일러야지. 소리나 빽빽 지르고. 밤새도록 작업한 거 집어 던지거나 하고, 당신더러 하라고 했으면 한 장도 못했을 걸.

최 PD　(버럭) 너 뭐야? 돌겠다, 정말. 송작가! 동생 왜 저래?

송희주　죄송합니다. (유미리에게) 들어가.

유미리 (무시하고) 어른이라고 다 어른인가? 어른다워야 어른이 지. 그게 힘들면 어른 흉내라도 내세요.

최 PD 내 나이가 마흔여덟이야. 자네만한 자식이 있어.

유미리 (여유있게) 나이 많은 것도 자랑이세요? 남의 집에 연락 도 없이 불쑥불쑥. 어리다고 반말이나 찍찍 해대고. 그 나이 먹도록 뭘 배웠나 몰라.

최 PD 이건 뭐, 말이 말 같아야 대꾸를 하지.

유미리 당장 사과하세요.

최 PD 송작가. 사태 파악 안 돼? 동생이 위, 아래 구분 못하고 망나니처럼 날뛰면 말려야지. 가만히 서서 구경이나 하 고. 이러니 회사에 민폐를 끼치고도 미안함을 모르지. 동생더러 당장 사과하라고 그래.

송희주 …

최 PD (송희주에게) 뭐해?

송희주 … 틀린 말은 아니라서… 뭘 사과하라고 해야 할지…

최 PD 자격도 없는 걸, 데뷔 시켜줬더니 지가 잘나서 된 줄 알 지.

송희주 그런 뜻이 아니라…

유미리 네 말 못 알아들어서 저 사람이 지금 저러는 거니? 뭘 그런 뜻이 아니야? '내 능력이다, 능력도 없는 사람 밀 어준다고 될 거 같냐' 왜 말을 못하니?

송희주 …

최 PD 송작가, 일 그만하고 싶어? 잘리고 싶지 않으면 처신

똑바로 해.

유미리　그럴 수 있을까요?

최 PD　내가 그럴 수 있는지, 없는지 똑똑히 보여주면 되겠네.

송희주　(용기내서) 얘기 끝났네요. 나가세요.

최 PD　후회 안 해?

유미리　그 말도 이해 못해요? 어머, 그럼 가르쳐 줄게요.

유미리, 핸드폰으로 전화를 건다.

유미리　(통화하며) 경찰서죠? 여기 사거리에 있는 오피스텔.

최 PD, 유미리의 핸드폰을 뺏어서 끊어버린다.
유미리, 현관으로 가서 문을 열고 기다린다.

유미리　길게 얘기할 필요 없겠죠?

최 PD와 유미리, 서로를 응시한다.

최 PD　재계약은 꿈도 꾸지 마.

유미리　마감 원고도 꿈도 꾸지 마세요.

최 PD, 현관문을 쾅 닫고 퇴장.

유미리 잘 봐둬. 나이만 믿고 사과할 줄 모르는 인간이 얼마나 추한가.

송희주 엄마는 날 위해 싸워주는 사람이었어. 유일하게…

유미리 그것 봐. 내가 아까 잘 할 수 있다고 그랬지?

송희주 그래.

유미리 너도 잘했어. (송희주처럼) 얘기 끝났네요, 나가세요.

송희주 내 입에서 그런 말이 나오다니… (피식 웃으며) 재밌었어.

유미리 처음에 네가 나한테 엄마 역을 해달라고 했을 때 나 사실 속으로 웃었다.

송희주 무대에서 널 처음 봤을 때, 마흔은 훌쩍 넘었을 거라 생각했거든. 엄마 그 자체였어. 나중에 나보다 어린 거 알고 깜짝 놀랐지만.

유미리 자기 나이랑 같은 배역을 맡지 못하고 머리에 하얀 칠한 채 나이든 역 하는 거 배우한테는 별 재미없는 일인데… 나도 네 덕에 안게 있다면 배우는 나이로 하는 게 아니라 연기로 인정받는다는 거.

송희주 엄마 역 해줄 사람이 필요해서 역할대행사도 찾아가 봤지만 너처럼 마음으로 내 엄마를 연기해주는 사람은 없었어. 물론 돈 때문이겠지만.

유미리 인정! 인정해. 두 달 연습하고 한 달 공연해도 내 손에 쥐어지는 건 십만 원. 너한테 받은 제의 꽤 괜찮은 아르바이트였지.

송희주 그럼 아르바이트 계속 할래? 기한도 남았는데…

유미리, 인쇄물을 주워 시체윤곽선을 본다.

유미리   아깐 네 편을 들었지만 사람들이 웹툰을 보면서 왜 그
런 말을 하는지는 이해가 돼.

유미리, 인쇄물을 송희주에게 건넨다.
송희주, 받아들고 시체윤곽선을 손으로 따라 그려본다.
그리운 얼굴을 만져서 기억하듯이…

송희주   잊고 싶지 않았어. 기억을 붙잡을 수 있는 건 기록뿐이
니까.

유미리   기억을 붙잡는다고 엄마가 돌아오지도 않고, 엄마와 네
가 보낸 그 시간도 돌아오지 않아.

송희주   너도 날 이해 못하는구나?

유미리   누구나 살면서 사랑하는 사람들을 잃어. 그렇다고 모두
너처럼 행동하지 않아.

송희주   남들이 보면 날 이상하다고 하겠지. 아니, 어쩌면 손
가락질 할지도. 그런데 그건 내 불안을 위로하는 방
법이야.

유미리   멈춘 시간 속에 스스로를 가두지 마.

유미리, 떨어진 과일을 치운다.

송희주 두려워. 엄마가 없는 미래가.

유미리 무지가 공포를 낳는다더라. 한 번도 가보지 못했으니 미래가 불안한 건 당연해. 그런데 머릿속에 그리는 상상은 오히려 현실에서 느끼는 두려움보다 뻥튀기 되어 있을지도 몰라.

송희주 아니, 난 엄마가 있을 때, 단 한 번도 불안하지 않았어. 하라는 대로만 하면 모든 게 쉽고 완벽했으니까. 세상이 이렇게 많은 선택의 연속이라는 걸 왜 이제 알았을까? 눈을 뜨면 '일어날까, 좀 더 잘까' 같은 사소한 것부터 재계약을 할까, 말까와 같이 밥벌이와 관련된 모든 걸 선택해야 돼.

유미리 다들 그렇게 살아.

송희주 늘 신중했는데도 매번 오답인지 아무 문제없던 내 일상은 엉망이 됐어. 이젠 내 판단이 맞는 건지 확신이 안 서.

유미리 그렇다고 평생 다른 사람의 선택에 의지하고 살 수 없잖아.

송희주 … 내가 또 다시 안정감을 느끼는 날이 올까?

유미리, 송희주를 안으며…

유미리 널 믿어. 두려움은 마주하지 않으면 절대 사라지지 않아.

송희주　오랜만이야. 이 심장소리.

유미리, 쓰다듬어 준다.
송희주, 화들짝 놀라며 떨어진다.

유미리　이 정도쯤은 괜찮아.
송희주　씻을래.

유미리, 속옷을 챙겨서 송희주에게 준다.
송희주, 받아서 화장실로 들어간다.
물소리.
유미리, 음악을 틀고 주방으로 가서 설거지를 한다.

사이.

현관 비밀번호 누르는 소리.
아버지, 등장.

아버지　(얼떨결에) 여보!

유미리, 돌아본다.

유미리　누구세요?

아버지	아니, 자주 보던 옷이라… 기성복이니까 여러 사람이 같은 옷을 입을 수 있죠.
유미리	누구냐구요.

유미리, 음악을 끈다.

아버지	내가 먼저 물읍시다. 누구세요?
유미리	집주인으로서 당혹스런 질문이군요.
아버지	당신이 이 집 주인이라는 거요?
유미리	어떻게 들어왔어요?
아버지	문으로요. 아, 그게… 비밀 번호를 안 바꾸신 모양이군요. 음… 이거 실례가 많았습니다.

아버지, 퇴장.
송희주, 젖은 머리를 수건으로 감싸서 나온다.

유미리	수건 뒤집어쓰지 말라니까. 머리가 다 죽잖아.

유미리, 드라이기로 송희주의 머리를 말려준다.

송희주	아파… 살살…
유미리	관리하기 힘들면 아예 머리를 뒤집어서 말려. 볼륨이 살도록. 해 봐.

송희주, 구부려서 머리를 아래로 늘어뜨려 말린다.

유미리　비밀번호 바꿔야겠더라. 이상한 남자가 들어와서 나더러 '여보' 래.

송희주　(고개를 들며) 혹시 우리 아빠 왔어?

유미리　그건 모르지. 난 너희 아버지를 본 적이 없으니까.

송희주　어떻게 생겼는데?

아버지, 다시 등장.

유미리　(아버지를 가리키며) 저렇게.

송희주, 유미리가 손가락으로 가리키는 곳을 본다.

아버지　당신 누구야? 왜 남의 와이프 옷을 입고 있어?

송희주　아빠. 친구예요. 갈아입을 옷이 없다고 해서…

아버지　(유미리에게) 보기 싫으니까 그 옷 좀 벗지 그러나.

송희주　아빠, 우리 나가서 얘기해요.

아버지　(윽박지르며) 너 새벽마다 사고 현장에서 그 짓한다며! 니 엄마 죽은 지 반년이다. 이제 정리할 때도 됐잖아. 애도 아니고.

유미리　(엄마 말투로) 왜 그랬는지 먼저 물어주면 안돼요? 말할 때도 부드럽게. 제발, 좀!

아버지	뭐야? 니 친구 아니지?
송희주	나가서 얘기해요.
아버지	설명해. 니 친구가 왜 니 엄마 옷에 니 엄마 말투를 쓰고 있는지.
송희주	말해도 아빠 이해 못해요. 아니, 이해 안할 걸요.
아버지	엄마 놀이라도 한 거냐? 이런 정신 나간 것. 엄마가 필요하면 말을 하든가.
유미리	(엄마 말투로) 말하면요? 새장가 가시려고요?
송희주	그만 해. 아버지 보내고 나서.
아버지	(유미리에게) 자넨 끼어들지 말게. 분명히 돈 받고 이 짓 하는 거겠지? 아무리 돈이 좋아도 그렇지.
유미리	(엄마 말투로) 당신 머리로는 그렇게 밖에 생각이 안 되죠?
아버지	그 말투! 당장 안 고쳐? (송희주에게) 집으로 가자. 더는 널 혼자 두지 못하겠다.
송희주	싫어요.
아버지	그럼 결혼을 하든지. 선 자리 알아봐 놓으마. 적어도 남들한테 손가락질은 받지 않을 거다.
송희주	아버지는 늘 남들이 어떻게 보는지가 더 중요하죠. 어릴 때부터 그랬어요. 난 한 번도 아버지 눈에 찬 적이 없었죠. 항상 부족하고, 못마땅하고. 그런 날, 아버지의 자랑으로 키우기 위해 엄마가 그랬는지도 몰라요. 나의 하루, 나의 신념, 내 인생 모두를 플랜을 짜고 관리하

고. 그게 다 아빠 때문이에요.

아버지 부모가 돼서 자식한테 그 정도 기대도 하지 말라는 거냐? 다른 집 애들처럼 혼자 잘했다면 아무 문제도 없었을 거다. 기껏 돈 들여 공부 가르쳤더니 겨우 한다는 게 만화나 그리고 앉았고. 너보다 성적 낮았던 애들도 지금 다 자리 잡고 사는 걸 보면 속에서 천불이 나. 대체 네가 뭐가 모자라서?

송희주 아빠 눈은 항상 나를 평가하기 위해 바라보니까요. 그 시선이 날 숨 막히게 해. 한번만이라도 그냥 믿어주면 안돼요?… 아빠잖아요.

아버지 지금도 봐라. (유미리를 보며) 이게 제 정신 박히고 할 짓인가. 뭐 하나 마음에 들게 하는 게 없는데 뭘 보고 믿으라는 거냐. 이제 네 엄마마저 없으니 더 형편없겠지. 혼자 할 줄 아는 게 뭐가 있겠어.

송희주 내가 엄마 없이 아무 것도 못하게 된 그 시작엔 아빠가 있었고, 엄마를 죽게 한 것도 아빠야. 엄마가 사고가 나던 날, 그 날도 아빠가 딴 집 애들은 이랬느니 저랬느니 하며 비교만 하지 않았어도 엄마가 그렇게 뛰쳐나가진 않았을 거야. 차라리 나 같은 거 낳지 말지.

아버지, 송희주의 뺨을 때린다.

아버지 말도 안 되는 어리광, 이만큼 받아줬으면 그만할 때도 됐다. 그런 식으로 따지면 네 엄마의 죽음 앞에서 그 누구도 자유로울 수 없다는 것쯤은 이제 알 나이도 됐잖아.

송희주 (눈물을 꾹 참는다)

아버지 하고 싶은 일, 하면서 살 수 있게 해주자고 네 엄마가 얘기했을 때. 그래, 바로 그 때. 그 날부터 모든 게 꼬였어. 남들처럼 평범하게 직장 잡고 결혼해서 사는 게 뭐가 어때서. 네 엄마가 내 뜻만 따랐어도 우리 가정이 이렇게까지 되지 않았을 거다.

송희주, 더 이상 참지 못하고 눈물을 흘린다.

송희주 내가 못난 건 나도 아는데 그게 엄마 탓은 아니잖아.

아버지 자식이 못나서가 아니라 못나게 사는 것이 싫은 거였다.

송희주 그러니까 그게 엄마 탓은 아니라고요!

숨 막히는 정적.

송희주 다시는… 찾아오지 마세요.

송희주, 방을 향해 돌아선다.

아버지　나도 무섭다.

송희주, 걸음을 멈춘다.

아버지　네 엄마가 죽고 나니까 뭐부터 해야 할지 모르겠다. 아침을 뭘 먹을지 동창회에 어떤 옷을 입고 나갈지 가르쳐주는 사람을 잃었어. 너무 오랫동안 고민하지 않았던 일이라 어색하다.

송희주　아빤 어른이잖아요.

아버지　아니, 나도 엄마가 보고 싶다. 너만 그런 게 아니란 말이다. 그런데 어쩌니. 나의 엄마도, 네 엄마도 가고 없는데. 너도 날 봐주면 안 되겠니?

송희주　…

아버지, 송희주의 뒷모습을 한참 바라본다.

아버지　기다리마.

송희주, 방으로 들어간다.

유미리　(엄마 말투로) 시간을 주세요. 대답하라고 몰아친다고 금방 답할 수 있는 게 아니잖아요. 다 커서 어른으로 보일지 모르지만 아직 희주 어려요.

아버지, 깊은 한숨.

책상에 놓인 액자에 눈길이 머문다.

아버지, 다가가서 액자를 손으로 쓸어내린다.

아버지   (사진을 보며) 처음 만났을 때도 이렇게 환하게 웃었지,
당신은… 많이 어렸어. 당신도 나도. 고작 스물일곱이
뭘 알았겠나. 저 녀석이 처음이라 아버지가 날 키운 방
식 그대로 하면 되는 줄 알았지. 돌이켜보면 이해받지
못한 내 어린 시절은 온통 상처투성이인데… 그걸 알면서
도 희주한테 똑같이 했어.

유미리   알고도 못하는 게 사람이에요. 당신이 아버지를 이해한
것처럼 언젠가 희주도 그 마음 알아주는 날이 오겠죠.
시간이 걸리겠지만.

아버지, 액자를 책상 위에 내려놓는다.

아버지   명함 한 장 주겠소?

유미리, 의아하게 바라본다.

아버지   다 아는 마당에 뭘 더 숨기겠나. 보다시피 저 녀석이 내
전화를 자꾸 피해요. 그래도 하나 밖에 없는 딸자식이
라고 모른 척이 안 돼. 그 쪽도 자식 낳아서 키워 보면

알거요.

유미리 바빠서 그랬을 거예요.

아버지 애써주는 건 고맙지만 나, 그 정도 눈치는 있는 사람이요.

유미리, 종이에 이름과 연락처 적는다.

유미리 (건네며) 필요성을 못 느껴서.

아버지, 받아서 주머니에 잘 챙겨 넣는다.

아버지 하나만 더 부탁합시다.

유미리 어렵지 않다면요.

아버지 (망설이다가) 인터넷 댓글 말이요. 어제나 오늘이나 다 비슷한 내용이 올라오던데.

유미리 간혹 옹호하는 댓글도 몇 개 있어요. 그런 분들은 참 고맙죠.

유미리, 순간 무언가 떠오른 듯 아버지를 바라본다.

아버지 다 쓸데없는 내용이니 우리 희주가 안 봤으면 좋겠는데… 특별한 게 있으면 내가 그 쪽한테 알려주리다. 들어줄 수 있겠소?

유미리 아… 물론이죠.

아버지 내 딸을 잘 부탁해요.

아버지, 쓸쓸히 퇴장.

유미리 내 딸… 내… 딸… (아버지 말투를 따라하며) 내 딸 미리를 잘 부탁해요. (쓸쓸한 미소) 내 딸 미리를… 잘 부탁해요…

송희주, 방에서 나오면서 본다.
유미리, 인기척을 느끼고 돌아본다.

유미리 (서둘러 엄마 말투로) 따뜻한 우유 한잔 줄게.

송희주 그만하고 싶어.

유미리 쉬어. 쉬고 나서 다시 얘기 해.

송희주 아니.

유미리, 엄마 역할이 아닌 자신의 모습으로…

유미리 있어 달라고 했던 건 너야. 처음도, 조금 전에도.

송희주 아는데… 끝낼 때가 온 것 같아.

유미리 상실감이 더 클 거야. 그래도 괜찮아?

송희주 아버지를 봐주고 싶어졌어. 한번쯤은 그래줘야 될 것 같아. 그래야 맞설 수 있을 테니까. 네가 말한 두려움.

송희주, 인쇄물을 찢는다.

송희주 엄마가 나를 슬픔과 고통에 맞서게 가르쳤다면 나는 좀 더 빨리 어른이 됐을까? 그랬다면 지금 덜 힘들었을 텐데…

유미리 같이 있어줄게.

송희주 가라고. 돈 때문이야?

유미리 널 만나 내가 쓸모 있는 인간일지도 모른다는 생각을 했어. 무대에서는 이름 없는 무명 배우, 학교 다닐 때도 내 이름을 불러주는 사람은 아무도 없었어. 불러주지 않으니 대답할 기회도 없었고. 넌 모를 거야. 그게 어떤 기분인지. 내가 아무것도 아닌 것 같은 느낌. 사람들 머릿속에 '그런 애도 있었나'로 기억될 초라한 내 모습을 보는 거. 다신 겪고 싶지 않아.

송희주 난 네가 어른인 줄 알았어.

유미리 그래, 어른답게…

유미리, 방으로 들어간다.
송희주, 집 안 정리를 한다.
유미리, 옷을 갈아입고 가방을 들고 나온다.

송희주　잔금은 통장으로 넣을게.

유미리　네가 얼마나 행복한지 넌 모르지? 난 한 번도 날 챙겨주는 엄마를 가져보지 못했어. 언제나 나보다는 엄마 자신이 먼저였으니까. 내 손으로 구하지 않으면 아무것도 얻을 수 없었어.

송희주　두려움에 맞서지 못하는 건 나랑 같네.

송희주, 유미리를 안아주며…

송희주　우리 미리… 혼자 많이 외로웠겠네.

유미리　…

송희주　원한다면 내가 엄마가 되어줄게. 네가 나한테 했듯이 나도 너한테… 아주 극성스러운 엄마로.

유미리, 송희주를 본다.

송희주　선물이라고 생각해.

유미리　…

송희주　잠깐 기다려.

송희주, 방으로 들어가서 올림머리에 엄마 옷을 입고 나온다.
송희주는 등장하면서 엄마인 듯이 연기한다.

송희주 (엄마 말투로) 이번 오디션은 제대로 해.

유미리 너 정말 웃겨.

송희주 어른한테 존댓말 하라고 가르쳤다, 난.

유미리 진짜 하자는 거야?

송희주의 핸드폰이 울린다.

송희주 (발신자를 확인하고) 최 PD네?

유미리 내가 받을까?

송희주 아니.

유미리 뭐라고 하면 같이 화내고 사과 받아. 네 잘못 아니야. 한 번 해 봐.

송희주 됐어.

유미리 해 보라니까.

송희주 그만하라고.

유미리 처음부터 잘하는 사람이 어디 있어. 해야 늘지.

송희주 (소리 지르며) 싫다는 데 자꾸 왜 이래, 나한테.

송희주, 유미리 서로 놀란다.

전화벨 소리 끊겼다가 다시 울린다.

유미리 잘했어. 이제 전화 받고 지금처럼만 해.

송희주 (전화를 받으며) 여보세요?… 네… 네…네. (전화를 끊는다)

유미리　뭐래?

송희주　마감 날짜 지켜 달래.

유미리　성공했네. 그것 봐. 해보니까 아무것도 아니지.

송희주　(엄마 말투로) 어른한테 존댓말 하라고 했지?

유미리　네.

송희주　봐라, 얼마나 예쁜가.

유미리　배고파요.

송희주　늦게 먹으면 살 쪄.

유미리　차려주는 음식 먹고 싶은데…

송희주　내일 아침에 네가 좋아하는… 뭐지?

유미리　떡볶이.

송희주　속 버려.

유미리　그럼 달걀부침.

송희주　오케이. (다시 엄마 말투로) 네가 좋아하는 달걀부침 해 놓으마.

유미리　지금…

송희주　한 번 말하면 들어.

유미리, 입을 삐쭉 내민다.

송희주　오늘만이야. 다음엔 안 통해.

송희주, 주방으로 가서 달걀부침을 한다.

유미리, 반찬 이것저것을 꺼내놓는다.

송희주, 거울로 유미리의 행동을 지켜보며…

송희주   너 여배우야.

송희주, 달걀부침을 식탁 위에 올려놓고 앉는다.

유미리   (반찬을 가리키며) 저거.

송희주, 반찬을 숟가락에 얹어준다.

유미리   (다른 반찬을 가리키며) 저것도.

유미리, 급하게 밥을 먹는다.

송희주   내가 널 어디서부터 가르쳐야 되니? 좀 예쁘게 먹어라.
          (달걀부침을 올려주며) 열 번 이상 씹어. 하나, 둘, 셋… 열.

유미리, 송희주가 열을 세면 삼킨다.

송희주   옳지.

유미리, 송희주를 보며 웃는다.

그 모습 위로 시가 흐른다. 정채봉의 시 '엄마가 휴가를 나온
다면'

소리   하늘나라에 가 계시는
엄마가
하루 휴가를 얻어 오신다면
아니 아니 아니 아니
반나절 반시간도 안 된다면
단 5분
그래, 5분만 온대도 나는
원이 없겠다.

얼른 엄마 품속에 들어가
엄마와 눈맞춤을 하고
젖가슴을 만지고
그리고 한 번만이라도
엄마! 하고 소리 내어 불러보고
숨겨놓은 세상사 중
딱 한 가지 억울했던 그 일을 일러바치고
엉엉 울겠다.

식사를 마친 유미리와 송희주.

송희주	난 어른이 아니야. 난 어른이다. 우린 어른일까?
유미리	우린 어른이 되고 싶은 걸까, 되고 싶지 않은 걸까?
송희주	그릇이 싹 비었네. 내 마음 같다.
유미리	이 기억을 안고 평생 살아갈 수 있을 것 같아.

유미리, 식탁에서 일어나 가방을 들고 나가려한다.
송희주, 유미리에게 다가선다.

송희주	작별인사는 어떻게 할까?

유미리, 악수를 청한다.

송희주	(악수를 하며) 잘 지내.
유미리	잘 지내.

막 내린다.

An In-between Girl

Choi Se A

_____

Cast

Song Heeju   (29, female)
Yoo Miri   (26, female)
Father   (57, Song Heeju's father)
Producer Choi   (48, male)

Season

At the change of season

Stage

The inside of an officetel.
There is a webtoon workstation and a dining table in the officetel.
A picture of a middle-aged woman is hanging on the wall.
There is a mirror reflecting the whole living room in the kitchen.
The actors and actresses can come in and out through the front door.

Car horns are blaring in the dark.
As the horns die away, Song Heeju enters the stage singing ⟨A baby in an island⟩
She draws a dead body outline on the floor with white lacquer.
When she's done, she lies within it

Song Heeju   Mom⋯ A countless number of cars runs over my mom's death. Oblivion is said to be God's gift, but it's a horrible punishment to me because I don't want to forget it.

All of a sudden, strong headlights flashes and the sound of horns get louder.
A short time of dark change.
As the stage begins to lighten,

Yoo Miri, whose clothes and hair style are the same as the woman in the picture, is setting the table, exactly measuring ingredients on a kitchen scale.
Song Heeju is doing yoga in the center of the stage.
Her eyes keeps straying over to her mobile phone.

Yoo Miri   (Looking at Song Heeju reflected it the mirror) Hold yourself straight. Then, You can have a nice figure.

'Ding-dong', the sound of receiving a text message.

Song Heeju stopps doing yoga.

Yoo Miri (Looking at the clock) We still have some more time left.

Song Heeju checks the message.

Yoo Miri Fill the ten more minutes.

Song Heeju I want some rest.

Yoo Miri Being impatient doesn't make the result come out early.

Song Heeju ⋯ I failed.

Yoo Miri (Looking back at her) Did you get a phone call?

Song Heeju Text message.

Yoo Miri comes out to the living room from the kitchen

Yoo Miri What's the reason?

Song Heeju I don't know.

Yoo Miri They can't do that.

Yoo Miri makes a mobile phone call.

Yoo Miri (Talking on the phone) I'd like to speak with the person in charge of 〈Today's Webtoon Award〉. (Pause) I'm the mother of webtoon writer Song Heeju, who was considered for the award.

Song Heeju What are you doing, mom?

Yoo Miri (Talking on the phone) I heard my daughter failed this time. Didn't you still have to let us know the evaluation criteria? Your message says just failure. You should have informed us of the result in a polite manner. (Pause) I don't want to hear about it. Just tell me the evaluation criteria. (Pause) If it's hard to answer, let me know the judge's phone number. Hello? Hello? (Hanging up the phone) Damn it!

Song Heeju What did they say?

Yoo Miri Never mind. They just don't recognize hidden talent. Stupid guys. Let's eat.

Yoo Miri moves to the kitchen and sets the table.
Song Heeju sits at the dining table.

Yoo Miri Don't brood over such trifles. In fact, that's not a prestigious award.

Song Heeju ⋯ I want to eat salmon.

Yoo Miri sits down in the chair opposite.

Yoo Miri I'm not going to put fish on the table for the time being because of radioactive leaks. (Cutting chicken breasts into ite-sized pieces) I've prepared the meal in consideration of he recommended daily intake of five essential nutrients, rotein, carbohydrate, fat, calcium, and vitamin, so make sure o chew your food well and eat everything on your plate.

Song Heeju starts eating.
She reaches for a cup of water.

Yoo Miri (In a soft but emphatic tone) Didn't I tell you that drinking ater in the middle of a meal can cause digestive problems?

Song Heeju   Because it's too dry.

Yoo Miri Once you starts, it's easy to do next, and it grows into a habit. Listen to me if you don't want to regret it in the hospital.

Song Heeju eat some salad instead of water

Yoo Miri (Putting some chick breasts on Heeju's spoon) You told me the other day that you needed pictures of a traffic circle for background for your work, didn't you? I took pictures of it region by region and filed them. I put the file on the bookshelf, so check it out after finishing your meal.

Song Heeju   (Taking it as usual) OK.

Yoo Miri Oh, when I got the phone call from producer Choi, I told him to call you again in an hour. When you talk to him on the phone, don't tell him everything you have in mind without much thought. Just get right to the point and hang up the phone. You'd better keep your distance from supervisors. If you're too far from them, they won't be able to recognize you. But if you stay so close to them, you might cross the line that you must not cross. Keep in mind that if you can't draw a clear line between public and private matters, you ight look rude.

Song Heeju   I know.

Yoo Miri   Is it due tomorrow, isn't it?

Song Heeju   You know about it better than me.

Yoo Miri   How much more work is there?

Song Heeju   Just adding colors to pictures…

Yoo Miri   Look, aren't you happy that you listened to me? You are not under the pressure of the deadline now because you've worked on it for three hours a day. You didn't stay up all night, so you have a smooth skin. Look how good your skin is! You can also feel it, huh?

Song Heeju   I got a facial yesterday.

Yoo Miri   (Ignoring what Song Heeju said) I've scheduled a meeting for tomorrow morning to make a contract for a full-length book. The boss doesn't like people who are late for appointments. We need to arrive 30 minutes before the meeting, so make sure you prepare yourself in advance.

Song Heeju   You don't care about my opinion again this time.

Yoo Miri   Have you ever been in trouble because you did the things that I wanted you to do? The only thing I regret, while bringing up you, is to let you do the job you wanted to do. Stop whining about how hard your job is because that's what you wanted to do. Once you've started your job, you have to see it through to the end. When you were young, I made you friends, took you from one private school to another to help you do well at school, waited in line so early in the morning to keep a seat in the library for you, spent what little money I had feeding and dressing you. Do you think I did all of the things just to see you struggling at the bottom of the ladder? Why did I do such things? That was all for your sake. I didn't want you to live like me. (Stroking Song Heeju's hair) I'll put it all back.

Song Heeju puts her spoon down on the table.

Song Heeju (In a whisper) I'm a failure to you.

Yoo Miri You are not to say the word failure with easy. It's not over. I won't let it go this way.

Song Heeju (Standing up) Let me get some rest.

Yoo Miri The deadline is just around the corner.

Song Heeju (Moving to the living room) I'd like to take a break.

Yoo Miri clears the table.

Yoo Miri Then, do it as you please.

Song Heeju stars at Yoo Miri.
Yoo Miri says in her own tone.

Yoo Miri Go get some rest. Go ahead.

Song Heeju (With a frosty face) My mom didn't say like that.

Yoo Miri I mean, you know, you said you were tired, so I think taking a short break isn't really a big deal.

Song Heeju I paid you to act like my mom, but that doesn't mean that you can shoot off your mouth.

Yoo Miri I can't understand you. Yes, you pay me, so I can do exactly as much as I get paid. But, you makes me feel heavy and suffocated. You also know it's difficult for you to live as your mom wants. Then, why do you want to keep doing this stupid thing?

Song Heeju I guess our deal is over.

Song Heeju enters her room.

Yoo Miri I mean you're grown-up, so I hope you live your life as you want.

Song Heeju in the room···

Song Heeju (Sound) I said it was over. Go.

Yoo Miri (Mumbling to herself) I have nowhere to go. (Facing the door) OK, I got it. Let me do it again. You know, contract is contract, so both of us have to abide by the contract. Do you think it's easy to meet someone like me?

Song Heeju gives no answer.

Yoo Miri (In the tone of Heeju's mom) Heeju, open the door. Can't you hear me?

Song Heeju in the room still doesn't respond.
At this moment, 'Ding-dong', the sound of the chime bell.
Several times, fast and harshly

Yoo Miri (Looking at the interphone and in the tone of Heeju's mom) Who is it?

Producer Choi (In a fiery tone) Open the door, Ms. Song.

Yoo Miri Tell me who you are first.

Producer Choi Are you kidding me? Open up right now!

Yoo Miri I said "Tell me who you are first."

> Song Heeju comes out of the room.
> Producer Choi knocks on the door.

Yoo Miri (In the tone of Heeju's mom) Such a rude guy. Take no
notice of him.

Song Heeju (Looking at the interphone) He is the producer I work
with.

Yoo Miri Don't worry. I'll act well.

Song Heeju You don't have to. If you do so, he'll notice you're just acting.

> Song Heeju opens the door.
> Producer Choi comes onstage.

Producer Choi (Bursting into a fit of anger) How could you do your
job like that?

Song Heeju …

Yoo Miri (In the tone of Heeju's mom) Phew, Ignorant.

Producer Choi Who? … Me?

> Song Heeju puts a stop to Yoo Miri's talking
> Producer Choi looks alternately at Song Heeju and Yoo Miri.

Song Heeju   (Looking at and talking to Yoo Miri quickly) Get some fruit.

Yoo Miri moves into the kitchen.

Producer Choi   (Staring Yoo Miri up and down) You have an unusual taste! I almost mistook her for your mom.

Song Heeju   She's my relative. (Changing the subject) The deadline is a few days away… Well, you've come to talk about a next book?

Producer Choi   Next? There would no 'next' if you go this way. No next!

Producer Choi takes out some papers he has brought.

Producer Choi   (Point at a paper) Here, (Turning the page) here, (Turning the page) here, (Turning the page) here.

Song Heeju examines the printed materials.
Yoo Miri watches what's happening in the living reflected in the mirror, peeling some fruit.

Producer Choi   I told you to revise the manuscripts, but why did you stick to them?

Song Heeju   …

Producer Choi   Ms. Song, Am I working with my boss?

Song Heeju shakes her head so slightly that producer Choi can't notice it.

Producer Choi   I already told you last time. You can't deal with this kind of subject. (Looking like a threatening attitude and slamming the printed materials on the desk) This doesn't match the story or meet the demand of the times. This isn't an advance hint either. I am asking why you insist on adding the dead body outline to every episode.

Song Heeju   ⋯

Producer Choi   Do I look like a fool to you?

Song Heeju   ⋯

Producer Choi   Please give an answer to my question.

Song Heeju   ⋯

Producer Choi   Oh, OK. How will you respond to online readers' request that the cartoon be discontinued. They think you are insane. All our staff are in big trouble because of you.

Song Heeju   ⋯

Producer Choi   There must be some reason behind your obstinacy. Otherwise, are you giving me a hard time on purpose because of the accident last time?

Song Heeju   ⋯

Producer Choi   We're not doing this just for fun.

Producer Choi pats Song Heeju a pat on the shoulder with the materials.

Producer Choi   If you are an adult, you should behave like one.

Producer Choi scatters the materials he's holding all over the floor.
Pieces of paper are scattered on the floor.
Song Heeju hardens her face.

Producer Choi   Did you draw this body outline of you mom, didn't you? Why do you keep drawing the outlines of your mom who already died? That gives me goose bumps. Please pick yourself now, okay?

Song Heeju   …

Producer Choi   Considering your position as a writer, I'll stop here to save your face. Unlike me, other producers would have throw the materials into the trash can.

Song Heeju squats down to collects the papers scattered on the floor.
Producer Choi tramples on the materials.
Song Heeju feels insulted but just lowers her head, bearing the insult.
Producer Choi sits down to make eye contact with Song Heeju.

Producer Choi   (Laying his hand on Song Heeju's shoulder) Don't do anything stupid any more. Let's make money. Money.

Song Heeju   …

Producer Choi A budding writer like you should be obedient. Did you expect to see something different? If you want to make it as a writer, you should listen to me.

Song Heeju ···

Producer Choi (Standing up) Don't make little of what I said to you. Today is the last day I treat you as a writer.

Producer Choi kicks the materials scattered on the floor.

Producer Choi Throw them away.

Yoo Miri drops the tray with fruit on it as she watches what's going on in the living room.

Yoo Miri (In the tone of Song Heeju's mom) How in the world could you do such a ill-mannered thing? Seeing that someone who doesn't know A from B about story writing sets himself up as a producer, his company is doomed to failure.

Producer Choi What? Excuse me?

Yoo Miri Don't be so mean to her here any more. Deal with readers who don't know anything about freedom of expression.

Producer Choi Shut the mouth. Are you teaching an adult like me.

Yoo Miri Well, You are not an adult at all in my eyes. If you think you are an adult, you have to reason with her on anything wrong like an adult. But you just yelled at her and threw away the manuscript she worked on all night. If you had been required to do what she did, you couldn't have finished even one page.

Producer Choi (Shouting suddenly) Who on earth are you? Are you driving me crazy? Ms. Song! What's wrong with your sister?

Song Heeju I'm sorry. (Looking at Yoo Miri) Go into the room.

Yoo Miri (Ignoring Song Heeju) Are all adults are like you? When you act like a grown-up, you are an adult. If you can't do that, just pretend to be an adult.

Producer Choi I'm 48. Even my kid is as old as you.

Yoo Miri (Staying calm) Are you boasting of your age now? You just broke into the house and talked very roughly although we are younger than you. Act as you should at your age.

Producer Choi Damn it! I don't want to talk back to you.

Yoo Miri Apologize for your rudeness right now.

Producer Choi Ms. Song. Don't you know what's going on here? You should have stopped your sister from turning on me if she says whatever comes to her head without respecting an elderly person. But you were just looking on. You don't seem to feel sorry for the firm you cause losses to. Tell your sister to apologize to me immediately.

Song Heeju …

Producer Choi (Talking to Song Heeju) What are you doing?

Song Heeju ⋯ What she said wan't wrong. What does she have to apologize for?

Producer Choi I gave you a job offer although you were not qualified. Then now, you think highly of yourself, don't you?

Song Heeju No, I mean⋯

Yoo Miri Tell him what you think clearly. Just say what's on your mind. Why are you hesitating to say "Yes, I'm qualified for my job. Do you think anyone incompetent can do what I'm working on if you back him up?"

Song Heeju ⋯

Producer Choi Ms. Song, do you want to quit your job? Behave yourself if you don't want to lose you job.

Yoo Miri Do you think you can fire her?

Producer Choi OK, I will show you clearly what I can do.

Song Heeju (Getting up her nerve) Then, no more to talk. Get out of here.

Producer Choi You'll be sorry for this.

Yoo Miri Can't you understand what she said? Alright, let me teach you.

Yoo Miri calls on her mobile phone.

Yoo Miri (Talking on the phone) Police station? I'm in the officetel at the crossroads.

Producer Choi snaps up Yoo Miri's mobile phone and turned if off.

Yoo Miri holds the door open for producer Choi.

Yoo Miri We don't need to say much, huh?

Producer Choi and Yoo Miri are staring at each other.

Producer Choi Don't even think about the renewal of the contract.

Yoo Miri Don't even think about the completion of the manuscript.

Producer Choi shuts the door with a bang and makes his exit.

Yoo Miri Remember this. How shameful it is to say just how old they are without making any apology for what they did wrong.

Song Heeju Mom fought him for my sake. Only mom…

Yoo Miri See huh, I told you I could do it well, right?

Song Heeju Right.

Yoo Miri You did a good job too. (Mimicking Song Heeju) Then, no more to talk. Get out of here.

Song Heeju I can't believe the words slipped out of my mouth. (Grinning) It was fun.

Yoo Miri When you asked me to act as your mom, I just laughed in my sleeve at first.

Song Heeju   When I saw you first on the stage, I thought you passed way over the age of 40.

Yoo Miri (Thinking she got it wrong) What?

Song Heeju   You are the mom. Later when I knew that you were younger than me, I was at a loss for words.

Yoo Miri With no opportunity to play a character of my age, I just acted like an elderly woman with hair dyed grey. No actress would like it. What I learned from you is that performers on stage are not recognized by their age but their acting skills.

Song Heeju   To find someone who would act like my mom, I visited an acting agency. But there was no one there who played as earnestly as you. Of course, you did it because of money though.

Yoo Miri You bet. I agree. I got just 100 bucks after two-month practice and one-month performance. This role-play you suggested to me is a decent part time job.

Song Heeju   Then, do you want to keep going? We still have some more days before the contract ends.

Yoo Miri picks up the manuscript and looks at the dead body outline drawn on it.

Yoo Miri I took your side earlier, but I think I can understand online readers why they comment on your cartoon like that.

Yoo Miri hands the manuscript to Song Heeju.
Song Heeju takes it and her finger follows the outline.
It looks like the face of her loved one flashes through her mind.

Song Heeju   I don't want to forget her. The only thing that can make me keep the memories is the records.

Yoo Miri   Even though you can keep the memories, your mom won't be able to come back to you and you can't turn back the time you spent with your mom.

Song Heeju   Even you don't understand me, do you?

Yoo Miri   Everyone loses their loved ones in their lives. Nevertheless, all of them don't behave like you.

Song Heeju   People might think me to be a strange woman. Well, they will go so far as to point at me. But that's the way I ease fear.

Yoo Miri   Don't confine yourself in the past.

Yoo Miri puts away the fallen fruit.

Song Heeju   I'm scared of the future with no my mom.

Yoo Miri   It's said that ignorance bears fear. No wonder you are worried about the future because you've never been there yet. But imagination may make the fear greater than the reality.

Song Heeju   No, when I lived with my mom, I wasn't scared of the future at all. Everything was easy and perfect when I did what my mom told me to do. Why did it take so long for me to realize that the world is full of choices that we have to make every day. From trivial stuff like buying a holiday gift for a boss to a means of livelihood like deciding whether to renew the contract, everything is a matter of choice.

Yoo Miri   That's how we live.

Song Heeju   I was careful to make choices, but I was wrong all the time and my life was screwed up. Now, I'm not confident of my decision.

Yoo Miri   For all that, you can't live for the rest of your life relying on other people's choices.

Song Heeju   I wonder the days will come when I feel a sense of stability.

Yoo Miri hugs Song Heeju.

Yoo Miri   Trust yourself. Fear will never disappear unless you squarely face it.

Song Heeju   It's been a long time. The beating of the heart.

Yoo Miri stokes down her hair.
Song Heeju is startled at that and stays away from Yoo Miri.

Yoo Miri This is OK.

Song Heeju I' ll take a bath.

> Yoo Miri gets Song Heeju some underwear.
>
> Song Heeju takes it and goes into the bathroom.
>
> The sound of water.
>
> Yoo Miri turns on music and moves into the kitchen to do the dishes.
>
> Interval.
>
> The sound of entering the code number for the front door.
>
> Song Heeju' s father enters the stage.

Father (In the confusion of the moment) Honey!

> Yoo Miri looks back at him.

Yoo Miri Who are you?

Father Oh, your clothes looks familiar to me. I mean, no, no, no. Right, since your clothing is ready-made, many people can wear the same clothes as you

Yoo Miri I' m asking who you are.

> Yoo Miri turns off the music.

Father Let me ask first. Who are you?

Yoo Miri That' s an embarrassing question for the landlady.

Father   You mean you are the own of this house?

Yoo Miri   How could you enter the house?

Father   Through the door. Oh, I mean··· You haven't changed
the code number yet, have you? Well, I'm sorry to cause
you some trouble.

Father makes his exit.
Song Heeju comes out of the bathroom with her wet hair
covered with a towel.

Yoo Miri   I told you not to cover wet hair with a towel. Your hair
gets stuck.

Yoo Miri drys Song Heeju's hair with a hair dryer.

Song Heeju   Ouch··· Come on···

Yoo Miri   If you don't want to care about your hair, dry your hair
inside out to volumize it. Try it.

Song Heeju bends over and hangs down her hair to dry it.

Yoo Miri   You have to change the code number for the front door.
A strange guy came and called me honey.

Song Heeju   (Hoing up her head) Did you happen to see my father?

Yoo Miri   I don't know. I haven't seen your father before.

Song Heeju   What does he look like?

> Father reenters the stage.

Yoo Miri   (Pointing to him) Like that.

> Song Heeju turns her head in the direction of Yoo Miri's pointing

Father   Who are you? Why are you wearing my wife's clothing?

Song Heeju   Father. She's my friend. She said she had nothing to change into.

Father   (Talking to Yoo Miri) I don't want to see you wearing my wife's clothes. Can you take them off?

Song Heeju   Father, why don't we talk outside?

Father   (Flaring out) I heard you go to the scene of the accident early in the morning every day. It's been half a year since your mom died. That gave you enough time to pull yourself together. You are not a child any more.

Yoo Miri   (In the tone of Song Heeju's mom) Can't you ask why she does that every morning first? And please speak softly, please.

Father   What's this? She's not your friend, huh?

Song Heeju   Let's have a talk outside.

Father   Tell me. Why is your friend wearing your mom's clothes and saying in your mom's tone?

Song Heeju   You won't be able to understand me. No, It won't be understandable.

Father   She's playing your mom? How stupid you are! If you need a mom, just let me know.

Yoo Miri (In the tone of Song Heeju's mom) What if she let you know she needs a mom? You want to marry again?

Song Heeju   Stop it. Let me see him off.

Father   (Talking to Yoo Miri) Don't cut in. She must have been paid for this, huh? You can't do this with money.

Yoo Miri (In the tone of Song Heeju's mom) Is that all you can think about?

Father   The damn tone! Can't you change it immediately? (Talking to Song Heeju) Let's go to my house. I can't let you stay alone any longer.

Song Heeju   No.

Father   Then, why don't you meet someone and marry him? Let me find someone you'll like. If you listen to me, you won't be pointed at by others.

Song Heeju   You always care more about how others look at me. You have been like that since my childhood. You have never been proud of me. I always fall short of your expectations, and I am an unacceptable daughter to you. Maybe, mom did all those things to make you proud of me. She made guidelines for my every single day, my way of thinking, and even my life and tried to control me according to the plans. She did all these things because of you.

Father   You mean even parents should not have any expectations for their children? Like other children, if you had taken care of yourself on your own, there wouldn't have been any problem. We spent a lot of money on your education. Then, look at what you're doing. You just draw cartoons. It makes me mad to see those who were worse than you as school work in better places now. What 's wrong with you?

Song Heeju   You always look at me to evaluate. Your cold eyes make me suffocated. Can't you let me do what I want to do even once? You are my father.

Father   See what' s going on here? (Looking at Yoo Miri) No person in his right mind would ever do something like that. How can I trust you as you have nothing to make me happy? I guess things would end up getting worse because you have no mom. I have nothing you can do by yourself.

Song Heeju   From the beginning, I couldn't do anything on my own without mom because of you, and also the person who made mom die was you. On the day when mom had a car accident, mom wouldn't have run out of the house if you hadn't compared me to other neighboring students who you said did better jobs at school than me. I wish you hadn't given birth to me.

Father slaps Song Heeju on the cheek.

Father   Don't act like a baby. I can't accept your childish behavior any more. If you say like that, you are old enough to know you also are to blame for your mom's death.

Song Heeju represses her tears.

Father   From the very moment when your mom said to me that we had to let you do whatever you wanted, everything was screwed up. Don't you want to have a normal job and get married like other people do? If your mom had followed my opinion back then, our family wouldn't have been broken up like this.

Song Heeju can't keep back her tears any more. She sheds tears.

Song Heeju   I know I am a stupid person, but this is not due to mom.

Father   What I hate about you is not your stupidity, (pause) but your miserable life.

Song Heeju   Anyway, that has nothing to do with mom.

Stifling silence

Song Heeju   Never come back here again. Never.

Song Heeju turns around toward the room.

Father   I'm scared too.

Song Heeju stops moving.

Father   I've had no idea what to do since your mom died. I lost the person who prepared breakfast and selected clothes for alumni reunions for me. I'm still uncomfortable to do that by myself.

Song Heeju   Father, you are a grown-up.

Father   Well, I miss your mom, too. You are not the only one who misses your mom. But what can we do now? Mom is gone. I have no one who cares about me except you.

Song Heeju   …

Father looks at Song Heeju's back.

Father   I will wait for you.

Song Heeju enters the room.

Yoo Miri   (In the tone of Song Heeju's mom) Give her some time. You can't force her to give you an answer right now. She is still young even though she looks grown-up in your eyes.

Father takes a deep breath.
Father turns his eyes on the picture.
Father approaches the picture and touches it.

Father   (Looking at the picture) When we met first, honey, you
beamed with a smile like this. You and I were very
young, just 27. We knew little of parenting. Heeju is our
first child, so I just thought that I had to bring her up the
way my father raised me. Looking back on my
childhood, my parents didn't identify with me. They just
hurt me. I thought I would be different from my parents.
Strangely, I treated her in the same way as my parents
did.

Yoo Miri People don't always do as they think. Like you finally
understood your father, someday Heeju will understand
you. It will take quite a while though.

Father adjusts the picture.

Father   Can I have your business card?

Yoo Miri gives a dubious look to him.

Father   When things have got to this state, I have nothing to
conceal from you. As you see, Heeju doesn't answer my
call. But she is my only daughter, so I have to care about

her. When you become a mom, you will figure out my feelings.

Yoo Miri Probably, she was too busy to get your call.

Father Thank you for taking her part, but I'm not that slow to catch on.

Yoo Miri writes her name and number on the notepad.

Yoo Miri (Handing it to him) I have no business card as it's hardly asked for. Here it is.

Father takes it and puts it in his pocket.
He gives his business card to Yoo Miri.

Father I have another favor to ask of you.

Yoo Miri If it's not difficult to do you a favor.

Father (Hesitatingly) The online readers' comments on Heeju's cartoon··· Most of them are very acrimonious every day.

Yoo Miri A few of them back up her work.

Father (Making a happy expression briefly) Really?

Yoo Miri Sure, One of the netizens is Song Palbong.

Feeling something strange, Yoo Miri takes a look at his business card. Gee! (Song Palbong is Song Heeju's father)

Father Besides that. Anything else?

Yoo Miri Well⋯

Father I want you to prevent Heeju from checking the reviews because all of them are not worth reading. If I find different comments, I will let you know. Can you do that?

Yoo Miri Yeh, Of course.

Father Please take good care of my daughter.

Father makes his exit lone desolately.

Yoo Miri Honey⋯ honey⋯ (Mimic Song Heeju's father) Please take good care of my daughter. (With a sad smile) Take good care of my daughter.

Song Heeju comes out of the room and looks around.
Yoo Miri feels indications of Heeju being around and looks back at her.

Yoo Miri (Suddenly changing to the tone of Song Heeju's mom) Let me get you a glass of warm milk.

Song Heeju I want to stop here.

Yoo Miri Get some rest. Let's have a talk again after you rest.

Song Heeju No.

Yoo Miri changes her role from Heeju's mom to her own self.

Yoo Miri It was you that wanted me to stay with you first. And you liked my role even a little while ago.

Song Heeju I know… but it's time to end it.

Yoo Miri You'll feel a sense of loss rather than happiness. Is it OK?

Song Heeju I'll have to forgive my father. At least once. Only if I do that, I can face fear. The fear you mentioned.

Song Heeju tears off the manuscript.

Song Heeju If my mom taught me how to deal with sorrow and pain, would I become a grown-up a little faster? If so, I would be in less trouble.

Yoo Miri I'll stay with you.

Song Heeju Please Leave. You want to stay with me for money.

Yoo Miri You made me feel that I'm not a good for nothing. I'm a nameless actress on stage, and no one called my name in my school days. I didn't make any answer because nobody called me. You don't know how I felt. It was like I was nothing. I didn't exist in anybody's memories. How poor I was! I don't want to go through the loneliness again.

Song Heeju I thought you were old enough to understand things.

Yoo Miri OK, let's stop our role playing.

Yoo Miri enters the room.

Song Heeju cleans up the house.

Changing into her own clothes, Yoo Miri comes out of the room with her bag.

Song Heeju   I remit the balance to your bank account.

Yoo Miri   You don't know how happy you have to be, do you? My mom didn't care about me at all. She always put herself before me. Unless I supported myself, there was no one to get me anything.

Song Heeju   As I tried to avoid fear, so you failed to face it.

Song Heeju hugs Yoo Miri.

Song Heeju   Dear my Miri, You must have felt so lonely.

Yoo Miri   ⋯

Song Heeju   If you want, I can act like your mom. As you did, I too can do it for you.

Yoo Miri looks at Song Heeju.

Song Heeju   Regard it as a gift for you.

Yoo Miri   ⋯

Song Heeju   Wait a minute.

Song Heeju enters the room, puts on her mom's clothes, combs her hair back, and comes out.

When moving to the living room, Song Heeju acts like Yoo Miri's mom.

Song Heeju (In the tone of Yoo Miri's mom) Make sure to show your talent in the audition.

Yoo Miri You are so funny.

Song Heeju I taught you to speak politely to elders.

Yoo Miri You really want to do this?

Song Heeju's mobile phone is ringing.

Song Heeju (After checking who's calling) Producer Choi.

Yoo Miri Do you want me to answer the phone?

Song Heeju No.

Yoo Miri If he is angry at you, be angry at him and demand his apology. You didn't do him wrong. You should do that.

Song Heeju That's Okay.

Yoo Miri Just do it.

Song Heeju Stop it.

Yoo Miri You may not do a good job in matching him at first. But you will be better if you keep taking a stand against him. Do what you did to your father to him.

Song Heeju (Yelling at Yoo Miri) I said no, then why are you pushing me to do that?

Both Song Heeju and Yoo Miri are surprised at Song Heeju's

yell.

The sound of the phone bell stopped and then the phone rings again.

Yoo Miri You did a good job to me. Answer the phone and do it to him just like that.

Song Heeju (Answering the phone) Hello? Yes···Yes···Yes··· (She hangs up the phone)

Yoo Miri What did he say?

Song Heeju She told me to meet the deadline.

Yoo Miri Good. See, dealing with him is nothing, isn't it?

Song Heeju (In the tone of Yoo Miri's mom) Didn't I tell you to speak politely to elders like me?

Yoo Miri Yes.

Song Heeju Alright, much better.

Yoo Miri I'm hungry.

Song Heeju A midnight snack makes you put on weight.

Yoo Miri I want to eat some food you prepare for me.

Song Heeju Tomorrow morning, I will make your favorite··· well··· what was it?

Yoo Miri Hot-seasoned rice cake.

Song Heeju It hurts your stomach.

Yoo Miri Then, fried egg.

Song Heeju Okay, (Changing to the tone of Yoo Miri's mom again) I will prepare some fried egg that you want to eat.

Yoo Miri I want to eat it now.

Song Heeju   Just listen to me. Don't make me repeat.

Yoo Miri makes up to Song Heeju for a fried egg.

Song Heeju   Okay, just today. Keeping after me won't work next time.

Song Heeju moved into the kitchen and make a fried egg.
Yoo Miri places some side dishes on the dining table.
Song Heeju looks at Yoo Miri reflecte in the mirror.

Song Heeju   You are an actress whatever other people say.

Song Heeju puts the fried egg on the dining table at which she sits.

Yoo Miri   (Pointing at a side dish) I want this.

Song Heeju puts the side dish on Yoo Miri's spoon.

Yoo Miri   (Pointing at another side dish) I want that.

Yoo Miri eats rice very fast.

Song Heeju   How many times do I have to tell you more? Eat it slowly. (Putting some fired egg on Yoo Miri's spoon) Chew it more than ten times. One, two, three··· ten.

Yoo Miri swallows it after Song Heeju counts from one to ten.

Song Heeju   Good.

Yoo Miri smiles at Song Heeju.
A poem is heard while Song Heeju smiles.
The title is If mom is at home on vacation by Jung Chaebong.

Sound   I couldn't be happier
if my mom who is in Heaven were
at home on vacation
for a day,
no, no, no, no,
a quarter of a day,
half an hour,
or only five minutes.

I would throwing myself
in my mom's arms,
look at her eyes,
touch her breasts,
and even once
call her Mom,
crying over

just one untold grievance

that I underwent in my life.

Yoo Miri and Song Heeju are finished with the midnight snack.

Song Heeju   I'm not a grown-up. I'm a grown-up. Are we grown-ups?

Yoo Miri Do we want to be grown-ups or not?

Song Heeju   The bowl of rice is empty. It's like my mind now.

Yoo Miri I can live for the rest of my life with our role-playing kept in my memory.

Yoo Miri stands up at the table and is about to get out of the house with her bag.

Song Heeju comes close to Yoo Miri.

Song Heeju   How are we supposed to take leave of each other?

Yoo Miri offers Song Heeju her hand.

Song Heeju   (Shaking hands) Take care.

Yoo Miri Take care.

The curtain is pulled down.

한국 희곡 명작선 07

어른아이

초판 1쇄 인쇄일   2019년 1월 16일
초판 1쇄 발행일   2019년 1월 25일

지 은 이   최세아
만 든 이   이정옥
만 든 곳   평민사
           서울시 은평구 수색로 340 [202호]
           전화: (02) 375-8571(代)
           팩스: (02) 375-8573
           http://blog.naver.com/pyung1976
           이메일 pyung1976@naver.com
등록번호   제251-2015-000102호
 정 가   6,000원

※ 이 책은 사단법인 한국극작가협회가 한국문화예술위
   2019년 제2회 극작엑스포 지원금을 받아 출간하였습니다.